peggy

for Peggy and her feathered friends

Clarion Books
215 Park Avenue South
New York, New York 10003

First published in Australia in 2012 by Scholastic Australia.
Published in the United States in 2014.

Clarion Books is an imprint of Houghton Mifflin Harcourt Publishing Company.

www.hmhco.com

The illustrations in this book were done in ink and photo collage.
The text was set in ITC Novarese Std.

Library of Congress Cataloging-in-Publication Data
Walker, Anna, author, illustrator.
Peggy : a brave chicken on a big adventure / by Anna Walker.
pages cm
"First published in Australia in 2012 by Scholastic Australia."
Summary: "Peggy, a hen, has a life-changing adventure when a gust of wind drops her in a big city."—Provided by publisher.
ISBN 978-0-544-25900-3 (hardback)
[1. Chickens—Fiction. 2. Adventure and adventurers—Fiction. 3. City and town life—Fiction.]
I. Title.
PZ7.W15214Peg 2014
[E]—dc23
2013034562

Manufactured in China
10 9 8 7 6 5 4 3 2
4500471484

peggy

A Brave Chicken on a Big Adventure

Clarion Books
Houghton Mifflin Harcourt
Boston New York

Peggy lived in a small house on a quiet street.

Every day, rain or shine, Peggy ate breakfast,

played in her yard, and watched the pigeons.

One blustery day, a big gust of wind swept down through the clouds, scooping up leaves, twigs, and . . .

Peggy!

Peggy landed with a soft thud.
She was far from home.
She picked herself up, ruffled her feathers, and went for a walk.

P
S
ON FOOT PATH
S
Collins Street

Peggy saw things she had never seen before.

Peggy watched, hopped, jumped, twirled, and tasted.

FRIED CHICKEN
Bargain Sale

She even found a cozy place to rest that
reminded her of home . . .

Although it was not quite the same.

Peggy missed her home.
She tried asking for directions,
but people found it hard to understand her.

In the rushing crowd, Peggy saw a sunflower like the one in her yard.

She followed the sunflower.

The sunflower sat down, so Peggy sat down too.

Outside began moving. They were speeding away from the tall buildings.

When Peggy looked around, the sunflower was leaving the train.

Peggy hopped out of the train, but the sunflower was gone.
She watched the sky grow darker as clouds rolled by.
The wind was cold.
A flock of birds flew quietly overhead.

It was the pigeons.

The pigeons knew the way back to her yard.

It felt good to be home.

Every day, rain or shine, Peggy ate breakfast,

played in her yard, chatted with the pigeons . . .

and sometimes caught the train to the city.